This igloo book belongs to:

....

Contents

igloobooks
.com

Published in 2012
by Igloo Books Ltd
Cottage Farm
Sywell
Northants
NN6 0BJ
www.igloobooks.com

FIR003 0712
10 9 8 7 6 5 4 3
ISBN: 978-0-85780-269-9

Printed and manufactured in China
Illustrated by Mike Garton
Stories by Jenny Woods

5 Minute Tales
Bedtime Stories

igloobooks
.com

The King Who Couldn't Sleep

It was bedtime at the palace. The queen had been out all day, shopping for a new crown and she was very tired. She even nodded off during pudding and woke up with her face in a bowl of ice cream. It was definitely time to go to bed. "Goodnight, dear," she said, giving the king a strawberry and vanilla kiss.

The king, however, wasn't a bit tired.

He brushed his teeth, put on his pyjamas and snuggled down in his royal bed with his teddy bear. However, the king could not get to sleep. He tossed and turned, wriggled and jiggled, fidgeted and fussed.

"It's no good," he sighed wearily. "I'm just not sleepy. Perhaps someone in the castle can help." So, he climbed out of bed and crept downstairs.

5

At the bottom of the stairs, he met the royal treasure keeper, who was weighed down with bags of jewels and stacks of gold coins. "I can't get to sleep," complained the king.

"I know just the thing to help you," said the treasure keeper. "Follow me." He took the king to the treasure chamber and gave him a soft, yellow cloth.

The king looked at the polishing cloth and smiled. "Oh, what a lovely blankie!" he said. "Can I cuddle it? I'm sure that will help me get to sleep."

"Erm, no, your majesty," explained the treasure keeper. "It's not a blanket, it's a cleaning cloth for polishing all the coins and jewels. I always doze off while I'm cleaning the royal treasure."

The king polished for ages and soon had the diamonds dazzling, the sapphires sparkling and the gold coins glittering like the sun. But he still did not feel sleepy.

"Thank you for finishing my work," yawned the treasure keeper, pulling on his nightcap. "I'm off to bed, goodnight."

"Oh, well," thought the king, "perhaps a snack will help me snooze."

In the castle kitchen, the cook was busy kneading dough to make delicious, fresh bread for breakfast. "I can't sleep," moaned the king.

"You've come to the right place," said the cook. "I always need a nap after kneading the bread dough. It's very tiring!"

The king was soon surrounded by a fog of flour, as he pushed and pressed the dough. Although he worked very hard, he still felt wide awake.

9

"Sorry you're not sleepy," yawned the cook. "Now the dough's done, it's time for me to say goodnight." Then, grabbing a glass of water, she set off for bed.

The king waved, but some of the flour got up his nose and made him sneeze. "Good - ACHOO! - night!" he sneezed. "I need some – ACHOO! – fresh air."

In the castle grounds, the royal gardener was cutting the grass.
"I can't get to sleep," wailed the king.

"I've got just the job for you," said the royal gardener, handing the
king a tiny pair of scissors. "Every blade of grass needs to be exactly
the same height," he explained. "It usually puts me to sleep after a while!"

The king knelt down and started snipping. He measured each blade of grass against his finger, to make sure it was the right height.

The queen, who had got out of bed, was most surprised to find the king crouched down, with his bottom in the air, poking a finger in the lawn. "Are you quite alright, dear?" she asked.

"I can't get to sleep," howled the king, "and no one can help."
"Don't be silly," said the queen and she took him indoors for a nice cup of milk.

The king took a sip of his milk. "I think I'll just snuggle down for a minute," he said. The queen was just about to read him a bedtime story when she heard a soft snoring sound. After all the activity, the wide-awake king was finally fast asleep.

The Lonely Owl

It was a clear, starlit, night and the moon smiled down on Owl's tree in the middle of the woods. But Owl wasn't feeling happy at all. Even the twinkling stars and glowing moonbeams couldn't cheer him up. Owl was feeling sad because he had nobody to play with. "All the other birds are asleep while I'm wide awake," sighed Owl. "It's just no fun being alone."

"I'll play with you," barked a voice from the bushes and out trotted Fox.
"Twit-twoo!" hooted Owl. "I won't be alone because Fox wants to play!"
"Catch me if you can," called Fox, speeding off into the undergrowth.

Owl launched himself into the air to search for his new friend. But he couldn't
catch up with super-fast Fox. At last, feeling tired, he flopped down to rest.

Just then, Mouse scurried by. Owl was so thrilled to see him, he swooped down at once. But before he could open his beak and ask Mouse to play, the terrified creature had run away. "Squeak!" said Mouse. "I'm going to run away, just in case Owl wants me for dinner tonight."

"Twit-twoo! Mouse is playing hide-and-seek," said Owl, in excitement, and he flapped his wings. "I love that game!"

So, with his wings over his eyes, Owl counted to ten. When he had finished, he shouted, "Coming, ready or not!" and flapped his wings furiously.

Mouse, however, was nowhere to be seen. Owl searched everywhere and was about to give up when he heard a rustle in the ferns. "Found you!" he called and and went to land in the undergrowth. "Ouch!" squawked Owl as he suddenly felt something prickly.

It was Hedgehog! He had been snuffling through the ferns, searching for his supper when Owl accidentally landed on him. "Help!" he squealed and, tucking himself into a tight prickly ball, he rolled away as fast as he could.

Owl was in a panic. Hedgehog's prickles had given him a nasty shock and he flapped around the forest.

Owl didn't see sly Fox hiding in the bushes. "Boo!" said the naughty fox and he jumped out at Owl.

"Aargh!" cried Owl in fright. He beat his wings, wildly, and flapped off towards the trees. "That's enough excitement for one night," Owl said. "I'm going home." So, he flew back to his hollow to smooth his ruffled feathers.

"I'll just have to get used to being on my own," thought Owl, sadly, wrapping his wings around himself.

Then, suddenly, a long, clear, note rang out. Lots of tiny voices sang together. Pricking up his ear feathers in amazement, Owl flew out into the woods. The branches were lined with his feathered friends.

"It's too early for the dawn chorus," said Owl. "So, what are you doing?"
"We saw what happened and thought you needed cheering up," cheeped Lark.
"Come and play with us."

The sun was peeking over the horizon, sending the first orange rays of daylight
through the trees. Owl lifted up his beak and, joining in the sweet birdsong,
he hooted in delight. "Twit-twoo! I've got friends to keep me company after all."

Counting Sheep

"Mum, I'm still awake," called Sam for the third time that night.
"Try counting sheep," suggested his mum with a yawn.
"But they're all fast asleep," Sam moaned.
"Not real sheep," laughed Mum, "shut your eyes and imagine them."

Sam settled down in his cozy, little bed and tried his best to picture sheep.

It was no good. Every time Sam managed to think of a sheep, it stuck its tongue out at him and ran away. "Mum, it's not working!" he shouted.

His mum answered with a loud snore. "Oh, well, I'll just have to come up with my own idea," Sam decided. So, he trotted out into the farmyard and looked around.

It was very quiet outside, but Sam could hear a clucking sound, coming from the hen house.

He knocked on the door and called softly to the hens inside. Suddenly, Mother Hen opened her beak and gave a loud *squawk.* "What do you want?" she asked.

Sam explained that he needed help getting to sleep.

"Come on, Sam needs us," clucked Mother Hen to the rest of the hens.

So, the hens followed Sam back to his room. One by one, they flapped over the bed, while Sam counted them. "One, two, three..." he began.

The problem was, as each hen fluttered across, it let out a loud *squawk*. "I'll never get to sleep with all that noise," thought Sam, so he thanked the hens and led them back to the hen house.

Those hens made such a din crossing the farmyard that they woke up the pigs. "What's going on?" they grunted. "We need our beauty sleep!"

Sam told them he couldn't get to sleep and the pigs agreed to help. "Pigs might not be able to fly," they oinked, "but we can trot round the bed while you count us."

Sam snuggled down under his duvet and got ready to count. But, as the first pig trotted by, he left such a stinky smell behind him, Sam began to cough.

When the next pig jogged round the bed, Sam's eyes started to water. "I'm sorry, I don't think it's working," he managed to splutter, trying to cover his nose.

When the pigs had gone back to their sty, Sam stood alone in the middle of the farmyard. "I feel wide awake, now," he sighed.

Henry the horse peered over the stable door. "It's no good counting horses because there's only one of me," he neighed. "When I can't sleep, I count all the rosettes I've won."

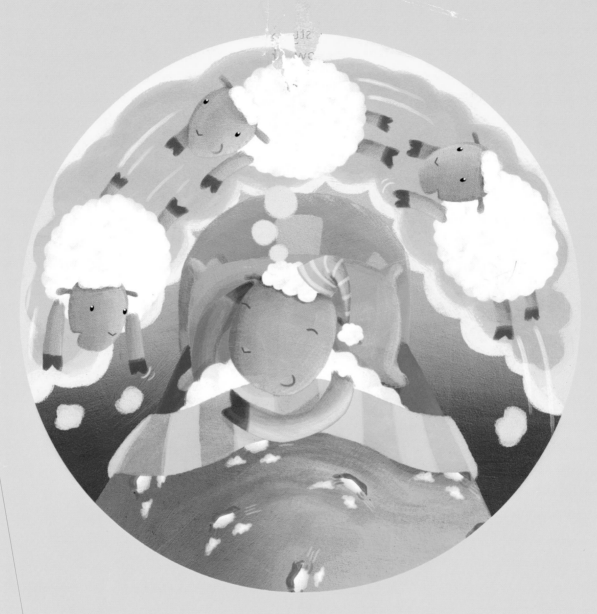

"I haven't got any rosettes," said Sam, "but I'm getting fed up of trying to go to sleep, Henry. I think I'll go back to my bedroom."

Tucked up in bed, Sam snuggled down and tried one last time to count sheep. "One, two, three…" he began. This time, the sheep didn't stick their tongues out and before he could count to four, Sam was fast asleep. Counting sheep had worked after all!

The Magic Present

Tom and Tia were very excited. Their uncle had brought them special presents back from his holiday. "You'll never guess what I've got for you," he said smiling and handing them a parcel each.

Tom and Tia eagerly tore off the wrapping paper. "They're cushions!" said Tia in surprise. Hers had stars on it and Tom's had stripes.

"They're special cushions," said Uncle, smiling mischievously.

The twins thanked him and ran upstairs, giggling. "What strange presents!" cried Tom, throwing the cushion onto the floor.
Tia threw hers down, too. "I can't see anything special about them," she said.

They both plonked down on top of the cushions. Then, something amazing happened. Suddenly, each cushion began to move.

31

The cushions whooshed up and flew out of the window and across the garden.
They whizzed over treetops and zoomed through fluffy, white clouds.
"Wow!" cried Tom. "Uncle's bought us flying cushions!"
"But where are we going?" gasped Tia. She wasn't sure she liked her new present.

At last, the cushions began to drift towards a big, green hill in the clouds.
Tom and Tia were very curious and began to explore.

"The ground feels funny," said Tia stamping her feet. "It's all smooth and shiny."

Suddenly, a huge scaly head rose up in front of them. Smoke and fire shot out of its nostrils. "It's a dragon!" yelped Tia, "We've woken him up."

The twins jumped back onto the cushions and flew away.

33

"That was close," said Tom, as the twins hugged each other in relief.
"I wonder where we're going now," said Tia.

The cushions went higher and higher, floating up through pink clouds until the twins found themselves in front of an enormous house.
"Come on," called Tom, "let's have a look inside."

The twins crept through the front door. In the corner of the huge room was a bed as big as a bus. Lying on the bed, in his pyjamas, was a giant.

"Friends!" boomed the giant, springing to his feet and making the house shake. "I'm going to keep you here so that you can play with me."

"Oh, no you're not!" shouted Tia. She grabbed her brother's hand and they both dashed back to the cushions.

The magic cushions soared through the sky. They flew over snow-capped mountains and whizzed past a beautiful rainbow.

Finally, they floated to the ground in a lovely meadow with a sparkling stream running through it. Over the stream was a little wooden bridge. The twins scampered onto it and peered down at their reflections in the clear water below.

"Urgh!" screamed Tia as the reflection of her face was suddenly replaced by that of an ugly troll. He looked at her with angry eyes.

"Who goes there?" bellowed the troll, jumping out from under the bridge. The twins didn't wait to find out whether it was a friendly troll or not. They hurried back to the cushions as fast as they could.

"I've had enough adventure on my magic cushion," said Tom.
"Me, too," agreed Tia. "It's much safer at home."
"Please take us home, magic cushions," they pleaded.

As soon as they had spoken, the cushions whizzed around and shot off into the sky. Before they knew it, the twins were back in their bedroom and someone was knocking on the door.

"Come in," they called and their uncle appeared in the doorway.
"Well," he laughed, "what do you think of your special presents?"

The twins looked at each other and smiled a secret smile, then rushed over to give their uncle a big hug.

"They're certainly not boring," said Tom.
"Best present ever," agreed Tia.
"They are magic!" the twins shouted together.

The Snoogle Race

It was nearly bedtime on planet Snoogle. But the little Snoogles weren't tired at all. "Bedtime!" cried Dad, but the naughty Snoogles had other ideas. "Come on!" they cried. "Let's go for one last whizz in our spaceships before bedtime!" Then, they all jumped up and down with excitement and dashed off to dive into their spaceships.

With a whizz-whoosh-swoosh they flew up into space. "Whee!" they cried as they vroomed past Venus, revving their engines and squeaking and squealing. The aliens there weren't very happy. They wanted an early night. But the little Snoogles took no notice and made even more noise than ever.

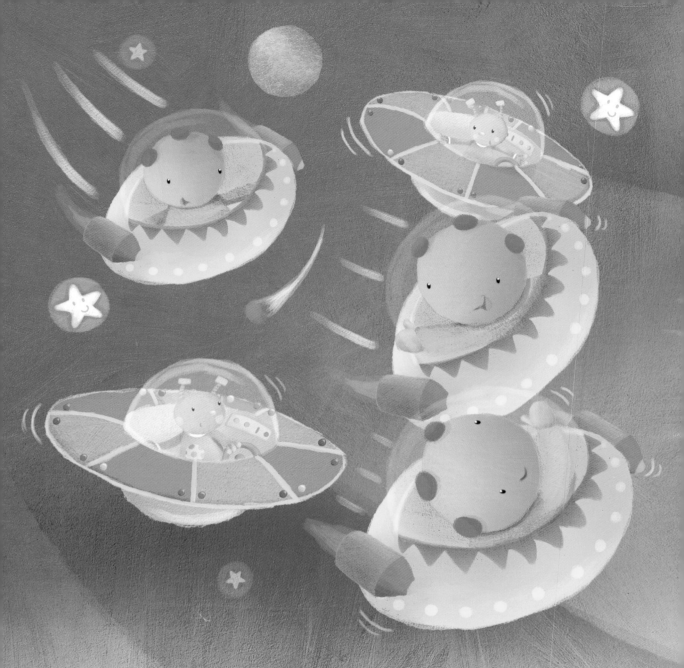

They circled round Saturn and motored towards Mars. Those naughty Snoogles were so excited, everyone had to dive out of their way. Then, suddenly, at Mars, some Martians appeared. They were bigger than the Snoogles and not very friendly. "Ha-ha!" they cried. "Isn't it time you were in bed? Bet we can get to planet Snoogle faster than you can!"

"Bet you can't!" cried the little Snoogles all at once. Secretly, they were a bit afraid of the Martians, but they weren't going to show it. In any case, it was too late to back out now. The race was about to begin. "1…2…3… GO!" cried the starter Martian. They were off!

Whoosh! Vroom!! The Martians shot ahead, but the Snoogles were on their tails. They edged closer and closer, nearly colliding with a comet and a big asteroid. Zoom! They raced ahead.

"Oh, no you don't!" cried the Martians. They went into warp speed and zoomed into the lead. There were spaceships dodging and diving, dipping and looping. They made a terrible racket, but it was loads of fun!

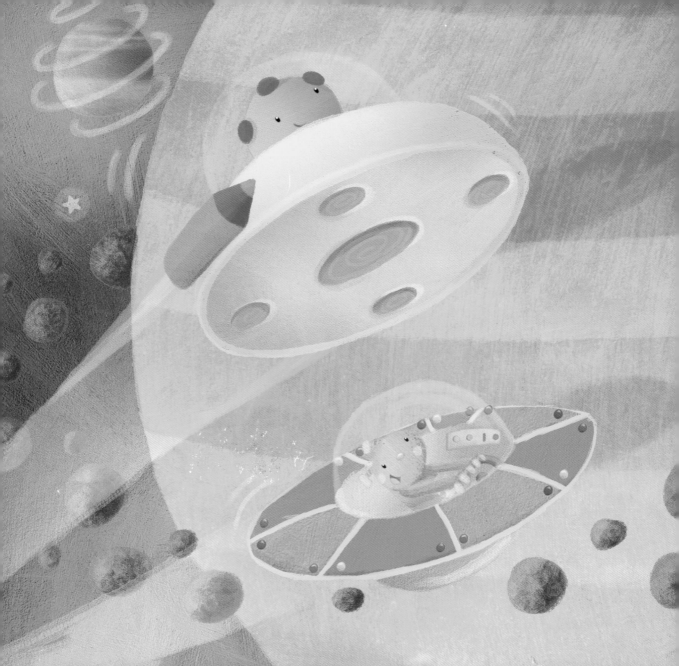

The Martians and the Snoogles were so busy trying to beat each other, they had forgotten all about getting to planet Snoogle and ended up taking the long way round. There was a terrible commotion as everyone circled around Saturn and nipped off to Neptune. Then they motored to Mercury and pressed on to Pluto. They went so fast, the planets began to spin the wrong way!

Suddenly, the Moon shouted "STOP!"

There was a terrible screeching as the Martians and the Snoogles slammed on their brakes.

"It's far too late to be racing around like this!" said the Moon. "You're making so much noise, you're upsetting the planets and the stars are scared. If the stars are scared they won't twinkle and that just wouldn't be right."

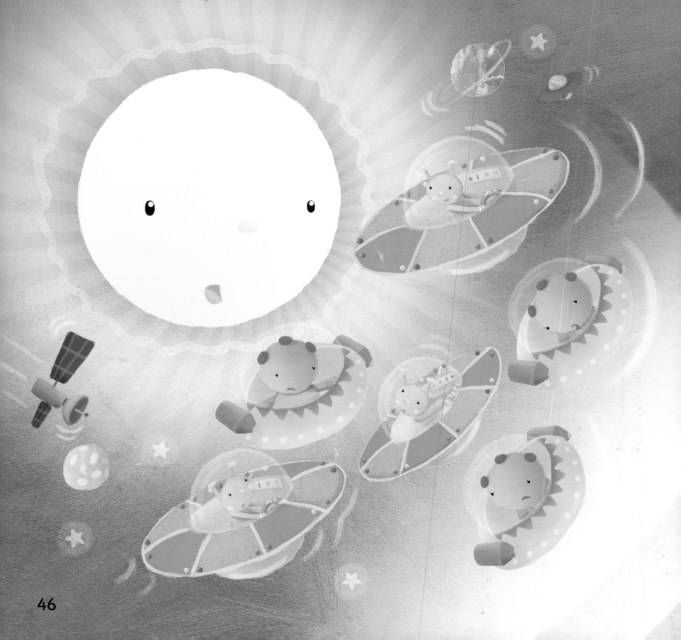

The Martians looked guilty and the Snoogles hung their heads. "Sorry, Moon," they said. "Sorry stars and planets. We just wanted to have some fun."

"There will be plenty of time to have fun tomorrow," replied the Moon, "when you've had a good night's sleep."

Everyone agreed. In any case, after all that racing, they were feeling quite tired.

So, the little Snoogles gave a big yawn and set off home to planet Snoogle. The Martians went back to Mars and everyone settled down. At last, the little stars twinkled in the night sky and all the planets began to spin the right way. A hush fell over space and everyone went to sleep. "Goodnight," said the Moon. "Sleep tight."